DEFENDING OUR NATION

DEFENDING THE SKIES:
THE AIR FORCE

Series Titles

DEFENDING THE SKIES:
THE AIR FORCE

FOREWORD BY
MANNY GOMEZ, ESQ., SECURITY AND TERRORISM EXPERT

BY
CHRIS MCNAB

MASON CREST

Mason Crest
450 Parkway Drive, Suite D
Broomall, PA 19008
www.masoncrest.com

Printed in the United States of America
First printing
9 8 7 6 5 4 3 2 1

Series ISBN: 978-1-4222-3759-5
Hardcover ISBN: 978-1-4222-3764-9
ebook ISBN: 978-1-4222-8020-1

Library of Congress Cataloging-in-Publication Data

Names: McNab, Chris, 1970- author.
Title: The Air Force / Foreword by Manny Gomez, Esq., Security and Terrorism Expert; by Chris McNab.
Description: Broomall, Pennsylvania : Mason Crest, [2017] | Series: Defending our nation | Includes index.
Identifiers: LCCN 2016053119| ISBN 9781422237649 (hardback) | ISBN
 9781422237595 (series) | ISBN 9781422280201 (ebook)
Subjects: LCSH: United States. Air Force--Juvenile literature.
Classification: LCC UG633 .M259 2017 | DDC 358.400973--dc23

Developed and Produced by Print Matters Productions, Inc. (www.printmattersinc.com)
Cover and Interior Design: Bill Madrid, Madrid Design
Additional Text: Kelly Kagamas Tomkies

CONTENTS

KEY ICONS TO LOOK FOR:

Words to understand: These words with their easy-to-understand definitions will increase the reader's understanding of the text while building vocabulary skills.

Sidebars: This boxed material within the main text allows readers to build knowledge, gain insights, explore possibilities, and broaden their perspectives by weaving together additional information to provide realistic and holistic perspectives.

Educational Videos: Readers can view videos by scanning our QR codes, providing them with additional educational content to supplement the text. Examples include news coverage, moments in history, speeches, iconic sports moments and much more!

Text-dependent questions: These questions send the reader back to the text for more careful attention to the evidence presented there.

Research projects: Readers are pointed toward areas of further inquiry connected to each chapter. Suggestions are provided for projects that encourage deeper research and analysis.

Series glossary of key terms: This back-of-the book glossary contains terminology used throughout this series. Words found here increase the reader's ability to read and comprehend higher-level books and articles in this field.

VIGILANCE

We live in a world where we have to have a constant state of awareness—about our surroundings and who is around us. Law enforcement and the intelligence community cannot predict or stop the next terrorist attack alone. They need the citizenry of America, of the world, to act as a force multiplier in order to help deter, detect, and ultimately defeat a terrorist attack.

Technology is ever evolving and is a great weapon in the fight against terrorism. We have facial recognition, we have technology that is able to detect electronic communications through algorithms that may be related to terrorist activity—we also have drones that could spy on communities and bomb them without them ever knowing that a drone was there and with no cost of life to us.

But ultimately it's human intelligence and inside information that will help defeat a potential attack. It's people being aware of what's going on around them: if a family member, neighbor, coworker has suddenly changed in a manner where he or she is suddenly spouting violent anti-Western rhetoric or radical Islamic fundamentalism, those who notice it have a duty to report it to authorities so that they can do a proper investigation.

In turn, the trend since 9/11 has been for international communication as well as federal and local communication. Gone are the days when law enforcement or intelligence organizations kept information to themselves and didn't dare share it for fear that it might compromise the integrity of the information or for fear that the other organization would get equal credit. So the NYPD wouldn't tell anything to the FBI, the FBI wouldn't tell the CIA, and the CIA wouldn't tell the British counterintelligence agency, MI6, as an example. Improved as things are, we could do better.

We also have to improve global propaganda. Instead of dropping bombs, drop education on individuals who are even considering joining ISIS. Education is salvation. We have the greatest production means in the world through Hollywood and so on, so why don't we match ISIS materials? We tried it once but the government itself tried to produce it. This is something that should definitely be privatized. We also need to match the energy of cyber attackers—and we need savvy youth for that.

There are numerous ways that you could help in the fight against terror—joining law enforcement, the military, or not-for-profit organizations like the Peace Corps. If making the world a safer place appeals to you, draw on your particular strengths and put them to use where they are needed. But everybody should serve and be part of this global fight against terrorism in some small way. Certainly, everybody should be a part of the fight by simply being aware of their surroundings and knowing when something is not right and acting on that sense. In the investigation after most successful attacks, we know that somebody or some persons or people knew that there was something wrong with the person or persons who perpetrated the attack. Although it feels awkward to tell the authorities that you believe somebody is acting suspicious and may be a terrorist sympathizer or even a terrorist, we have a higher duty not only to society as a whole but to our family, friends, and ultimately ourselves to do something to ultimately stop the next attack.

It's not *if* there is going to be another attack, but where, when, and how. So being vigilant and being proactive are the orders of the day.

Manny Gomez, Esq.
President of MG Security Services,
Chairman of the National Law Enforcement Association,
former FBI Special Agent, U.S. Marine, and NYPD Sergeant

CHAPTER 1

HISTORY OF THE U.S. AIR FORCE

The Air Force Memorial in Arlington, VA, honors the personnel of the United States Air Force.

B y 2016, the U.S. Air Force was nearly 70 years old, having been established in 1947. Although it is one of the youngest elements of the U.S. military, it is the most potent air force in existence today.

In December 1903, the pioneers of powered flight, the Wright brothers, flew the first heavier-than-air aircraft, a biplane called the "Flier." The flight at the sands of Kitty Hawk, NC, began the history of civil and military aviation and the history of the United States Air Force (USAF).

The Wright Military Flyer arriving at Fort Meyer, VA, in 1908.

Words to Understand

Airship: Large aircraft without wings, filled with gas, and powered by a motor.

Inexorable: Not able to be stopped or changed.

Tactician: Someone who is good at making plans to achieve goals.

For military **tacticians**, aircraft offered the ability to cross enemy lines at will on either combat or reconnaissance missions. The U.S. Army Signal Corps, the branch of the Army concerned with communications and surveillance, formed the Aeronautical Division on August 1, 1907. In 1909, it received its first aircraft, a later version of the Wrights' Flier, and by 1913, the Army had a fully operational unit, the 1st Aero Squadron. However, military aviation was still young. The Army relied more on hot-air balloons and **airships** to conduct its reconnaissance, as it had since the Civil War (1861–1865) and the Spanish-American War (1889). It would take a world war to change this way of thinking.

The Growth of the Air Force

In 1914, Europe was plunged into World War I, a war that raged across the continent, and it soon became clear that aircraft could make a significant contribution. Although the United States did not join the war for another three years, the government realized that it lagged behind the European powers, having few aircraft and scant resources. Even before war broke out, Congress established the Aviation Section of the Signal Corps on July 18, 1914. Nonetheless, this was weak when compared to the air forces of the warring nations, all of which had large units of combat aircraft. And when the United States entered the war in 1917, the government faced criticism about the lack of air power.

In response, President Woodrow Wilson formed the Army Air Service on May 24, 1918, and invested in its strength and technology. Many U.S. pilots had already gained air combat experience by flying with other Allied air forces or as part of the American Expeditionary Forces (AEF), which was established in 1917 and fought in the final year of World War I. Captain Edward V. Rickenbacker, for instance, became a true fighter ace, personally shooting down 26 enemy aircraft. Taking advantage of such experience, President Wilson passed legislation that brought the Army Air Service to a strength of nearly 200,000 men and 11,754 aircraft by November 1918. However, November 1918 was also the month in which the war ended, and the Army Air Service was dramatically cut back.

While the European nations involved in World War I had created separate air forces, the U.S. Air Service remained as part of the Army. On July 2, 1926, the Air Corps Act redesignated the Air Service as the Army Air Corps, and in 1935, all Air Corps units fell under the command of General Headquarters Air Force.

Edward V. Rickenbacker was the American "Ace of Aces" in World War I.

As with the Army and Navy, it was World War II (1939–1945) that revolutionized the Air Force. At the outbreak of war, the Army Air Corps had 24,000 personnel and 1,500 combat aircraft, still far below the strength of the European air forces. Realizing this, the U.S. government embarked on a massive program of expanding its air units. On June 20, 1941, six months before the United States actually entered the war, the Air Corps was renamed the United States Army Air Force (USAAF).

During World War II, the USAAF grew to an immense size, peaking in 1944 at around 60,000 combat aircraft, 20,000 support aircraft, and 2,372,292 personnel. U.S. industry also

Boeing B-17 bombers used during World War II.

turned out some of the best aircraft of the entire war. Aircraft such as the P-51 Mustang long-range fighter and the B-17 Flying Fortress bomber were vital in bringing enemy air forces and industry to their knees. By mid-1944, U.S. and Allied air forces had complete air superiority over both Germany and Japan. Indeed, it was U.S. air power that finally brought World War II to an end, when the USAAF B-29 Superfortresses dropped atomic bombs over Hiroshima and Nagasaki in 1945.

An Independent Air Force

World War II proved the value of U.S. air power. Although many units were disbanded as the conflict ended, the government recognized that the USAAF should have a new status. On September 18, 1947, the USAF was officially formed as a separate command and given equality with the Army and the Navy. General Carl A. Spaatz was the first USAF chief of staff.

As the world war ended, the Cold War began. After 1949, the year in which the Soviet Union tested its first atomic bomb, one of the main roles of the USAF was to defend against or deploy nuclear weapons. The Strategic Air Command (SAC) was created in 1946. Its mission was to launch nuclear-capable bombers against the Soviet Union in the event of a nuclear war. To perform this role, the USAF created new long-range bombers, including the B-36 Peace-maker and, later, the enormous B-52 Stratofortress. In the 1960s, SAC also took over control of many of the United States' intercontinental ballistic missiles (ICBMs), designed to be launched from silos on the U.S. mainland.

Nuclear-weapons deployment was only one aspect of the new Air Force. By 1950, it was back in conventional air-combat roles with the onset of the Korean War (1950–1953). In Korea, jet aircraft clashed for the first time in combat, with the USAF represented by the North American F-86 Sabre and North Korea by MiG 15 jets. The battle was close-fought—750 U.S. aircraft were destroyed in the war for over 950 North Korean and Chinese jets. During the 1950s the USAF steadily made the shift from turboprop aircraft to faster and more powerful jet aircraft, supersonic flight having already been achieved—on October 14, 1947, test pilot

In 1966, the B-52, which had been able to carry 51 bombs, was modified to carry 108 bombs.

Chuck Yeager flew his Bell XS-1 faster than the speed of sound. It is worth noting, however, that turboprops retain many transportation and surveillance roles in the Air Force even today.

In the early 1960s, the USAF became involved in another conflict in the Far East, this time in the troubled country of Vietnam. The United States was steadily dragged into the war between North and South Vietnam, and for over 10 years, the Air Force flew thousands of combat and supply missions.

The Vietnam War (1963–1975) was one of the greatest periods of technological development in the Air Force. Helicopters were the principal method of transporting troops and supplies, and combat helicopters armed with rockets and machine guns were developed. In the face of such lethal air defenses, classic aircraft, such as the McDonnell Douglas F-4 Phantom and Republic F-105 Thunder-chief, conducted missions over North Vietnam. Precision-guided bombs

F-105s preparing to take off on a mission to bomb North Vietnam in 1966.

and air-to-air missiles (AAMs) were used for the first time, with impressive results. The Air Force also conducted some of the heaviest aerial bombardments in history at this time. During Operation Rolling Thunder (1965–1968), for instance, USAF, U.S. Navy, and U.S. Marine Corps aircraft dropped more than one million tons of bombs over North Vietnam.

The Vietnam War was ultimately a defeat for the United States. The Air Force, however, had shown that it could achieve complete air superiority and was a powerful force for waging war. Following the Vietnam conflict, the USAF continued with what has proved to be an **inexorable** rise to technological dominance.

Refueling in midair.

In the 1970s and 1980s, new aircraft emerged, such as the F-15 Eagle, the F-16 Fighting Falcon, the A-10 Thunderbolt, and the E-3 Sentry. These aircraft brought new standards to military aviation with lethal advanced weapons, such as laser-guided bombs and the A-10's enormous tank-busting GAU-8 multibarreled cannon, which is capable of firing 75 high-explosive armor-piercing shells every second. The Air Force also acquired a large fleet of airborne-refueling aircraft and long-range supply aircraft, giving it the ability to fuel and resupply without touching down.

The Modern Air Force

For much of the Cold War, the U.S. and Soviet air forces had similar capabilities and strengths. However, during the 1980s, the United States' great industrial wealth let it leap ahead in technology, quality of personnel, and tactical training. A landmark was the emergence of the revolutionary F-117A "stealth" fighter, a jet that looks like something out of a science-fiction movie and that is capable of flying through enemy airspace without being detected by enemy radar. In 1992, the B-2 stealth bomber also emerged.

Brigadier General William Mitchell

One of the most significant figures in the history of the USAF is General William "Billy" Mitchell. He began a military career in the Army during the Spanish-American War of 1889. In 1915, he joined the aviation section of the Signal Corps and learned to fly in 1916. During World War I, Mitchell was an innovative and daring air commander in France. He was the first American airman to fly across enemy lines, and he launched the world's first major bombing attack, using 1,500 aircraft.

After the war, he gave the first demonstration of dropping combat troops by parachute. He also became assistant chief of the Air Service and argued vehemently for the creation of a separate air force. He retired on February 1, 1926, still arguing—and warning—that Japan's aircraft carriers were a threat to the U.S. fleet at Hawaii. Mitchell died on February 19, 1936; five years later, Pearl Harbor was attacked. Military officials suddenly recognized how visionary Mitchell had been, and many of his ideas were then implemented. In 1948, General Carl Spaatz, chief of staff of the newly created U.S. Air Force, presented Mitchell's son with a medal authorized by Congress that honored his father's contribution to U.S. military aviation.

General William "Billy" Mitchell is known as the father of the U.S. Air Force.

The 1980s saw the Air Force engage in many operations, including Grenada (1983), Libya (1986), and Panama (1989). Even after the end of the Cold War in 1989, when the Berlin Wall was finally pulled down, a year rarely went by without the Air Force being sent into action somewhere in the world.

In the Gulf War (1990–1991), USAF aircraft devastated Iraqi military forces and communications. Such was the efficiency of their bombardments that the land campaign to expel Iraqi forces from Kuwait lasted only 100 hours and cost few lives. USAF units operate in the Middle East to this day, but the Air Force has performed hundreds of other missions around the world since the end of the Gulf War, particularly in Europe, in the former country of Yugoslavia, between 1993 and 1999.

Today, the USAF is engaged in the war against terrorism, pounding enemy strongholds in support of ground-troop operations. The firepower, surveillance, and reach of the Air Force have attained such levels that no professional army in the world can stand up to its force in an open campaign. The war on terrorism is a difficult one for the U.S. military, but the Air Force is, as always, playing a major part in protecting the nation.

Text-Dependent Questions
1. What division of the army was the first to use aircraft?
2. Which world war was the first that the Army Air Service participated in?
3. What was the initial mission of the Strategic Air Command when it formed in 1946?

Research Projects
1. What was the U.S. Air Force's role in the Gulf War? How many missions were flown and what did they achieve?
2. Research the F-117A "stealth" fighter. How many missions have utilized this aircraft and why were they required for those missions?

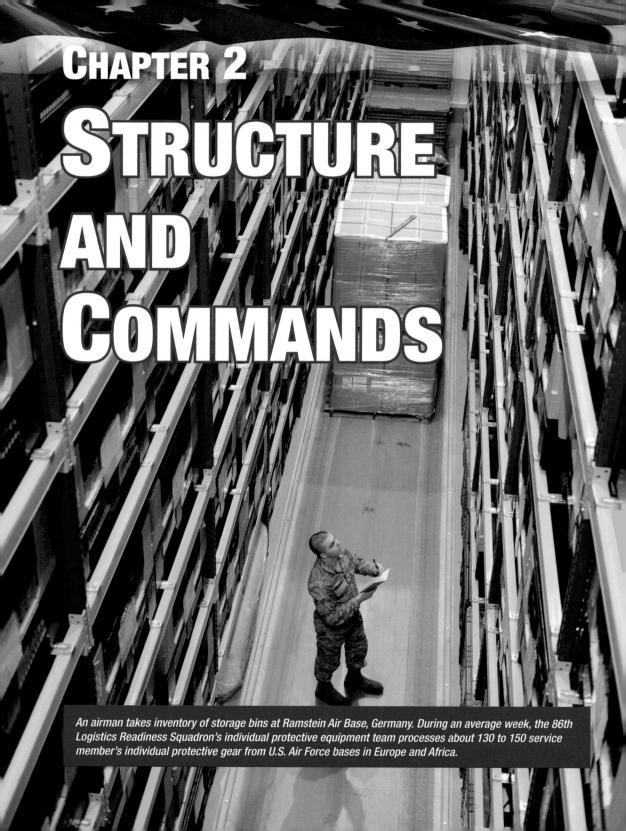

CHAPTER 2

STRUCTURE AND COMMANDS

An airman takes inventory of storage bins at Ramstein Air Base, Germany. During an average week, the 86th Logistics Readiness Squadron's individual protective equipment team processes about 130 to 150 service member's individual protective gear from U.S. Air Force bases in Europe and Africa.

The Air Force has undergone many changes over the last 10 years. Its command structure enables it to respond to crises in a matter of hours. Just like the poster appearing on the walls of many USAF bases says, "The mission of the United States Air Force is to fly and fight, and don't you ever forget it."

Although the Air Force has many other roles, this statement is still accurate. Since it was created in 1947, the USAF has been in the frontline of most U.S. combat missions around the world.

The Organization of the USAF

Like the other branches of the U.S. armed forces, the USAF is ultimately commanded by the President and the Secretary of Defense. Just below this level of authority is the commander in chief (CINC) of the USAF, who sits on the Joint Chiefs of Staff (JCS).

The commander in chief is ultimately responsible for Air Force deployments and operations. In a time of war, however, control of the USAF passes over to what is known as a Unified Command. A Unified Command contains elements of the Army, Navy, and Air Force and exercises responsibility for a particular geographical region of the world.

The Air Force itself is split into a number of commands—huge units that each run different areas of USAF operations. Currently, there are 10 major commands.

Words to Understand

Contingency operation: An operation that can be executed in the event that an existing operation fails.

Covert: Secret or hidden.

Infiltration: Secretly enter or join a group.

Air Combat Command (ACC)

The ACC is one of the largest and most important of the commands. It operates all of the USAF's warplanes—more than 1,700 combat aircraft. It has responsibility not only for fighter and bomber aircraft, but also for the deployment of air-launched nuclear weapons in the case of a nuclear conflict. ACC is based at Langley Air Force Base (AFB), VA.

Members of the Air Combat Command Honor Guard post colors at a September 11th memorial.

Air Mobility Command (AMC)

AMC's role is the rapid deployment of U.S. armed forces units around the world in support of operations, a job it does using fleets of long-range transport aircraft. It is based at Scott Air Force Base (AFB), IL.

During mass-tactical week the Army and Air Force unite to improve interoperability for worldwide crisis, contingency, and humanitarian operations.

Air Force Materiel Command (AFMC)

The AFMC was created on July 1, 1992. It is responsible for developing and maintaining USAF aircraft and technology, and giving the USAF the best tools of war. AFMC tests and evaluates new aircraft and weapons and employs around 90,000 personnel. Its headquarters are at Wright-Patterson AFB, OH.

Air Force Space Command (AFSC)

AFSC was created on September 1, 1982, and is headquartered at Peterson AFB, CO. With more than 40,000 personnel, the AFSC maintains and, if necessary, deploys, USAF intercontinental ballistic missiles (ICBMs), controlling approximately one-third of the United States' entire nuclear capability. The AFSC also launches military satellites, conducts space-based surveillance, and provides navigational facilities to military units on the ground.

Air Force Special Operations Command (AFSOC)

AFSOC specializes in **covert** or high-risk operations. Its main role is the stealthy **infiltration** of U.S. special forces soldiers using airborne means, but it will also deploy weapons when necessary. AFSOC has 12,000 personnel and around 100 aircraft, both fixed and rotary-wing (rotary-wing aircraft are also known as helicopters).

Pacific Air Forces (PACAF)

PACAF is a geographical command responsible for 100 million square miles (258 sq km) of territory between the west coast of the United States and the east coast of Africa. With more than 45,000 personnel and over 300 warplanes, PACAF can respond to crisis or conflict in any of the 44 countries in its region. Its headquarters are at Hickham AFB, HI.

3,523
0132
39,100 ft

3,552
0374
18,000 ft

3,553
0356
5,700 ft

3,629
2657
1,000 ft

SUTRA22
4051
37 ft

The Pacific Air Forces monitors aircraft that enter and leave training areas. The Joint Deployable Electronic Warfare Range has been used to support multinational and joint exercises at weapon ranges in Thailand, Australia, and Canada, and unit-level training in South Korea.

Air Education and Training Command (AETC)

AETC's job is to train future airmen and other personnel for service in the USAF. It uses 1,600 aircraft, 1,400 recruiters, and 28 squadrons to accomplish this task. Around 36,000 people each year complete the USAF basic training course at Lackland AFB, TX.

United States Air Forces in Europe (USAFE)

The USAFE has its headquarters at Ramstein Air Base, Germany. Using around 225 military aircraft and 35,000 active personnel, USAFE conducts USAF operations in Europe and Africa and also supports European NATO air forces when required. The USAFE has seen a lot of action over the last 15 years, using more than 180 aircraft in the Gulf War and flying many humanitarian and combat operations in Africa and southern Europe. This major command has played an integral part in several military combat operations since the 1990s, including Desert Shield, Desert Storm, Operations Enduring Freedom, and Iraqi Freedom. In 2011, this command also began attacks against ISIS groups in Syria.

Air Force Reserve Command (AFRC)

AFRC is the newest of the major USAF commands. It was created on February 17, 1997, and has the role of providing additional power to USAF missions when necessary. AFRC has 447 military aircraft, 99 percent of which can be brought into action within 72 hours. AFRC also contains many support units, such as medical, engineering, communications, and transportation teams.

Air Force Global Strike Command (AFGFC)

The AFGFC major command of the USAF is headquartered at Barksdale AFB, LA. The primary mission of the AFGFC is to provide combat-ready air forces against nuclear attacks and to support other combat commanders. Formed in 2009, it has approximately 31,000 professionals at work to uphold its mission.

Air Force Roles

The obvious duty of the USAF is fighting wars, but there are many different roles within this category. There are three main types of combat aircraft, each with a specific job.

Air National Guard

The Air National Guard (ANG) is the defender of U.S. airspace. Like the Army's National Guard, the ANG has a responsibility for federal and state defense, but it also provides 100 percent of the U.S. air-defense interceptor force and about 50 percent of the USAF's support duties. It is manned full time by civilian personnel, who have a military status within the ANG. In total, it has over 106,000 personnel and 88 flying units regularly deployed overseas. ANG aircraft flew combat missions in the Gulf War, and since then have been regularly used in humanitarian and contingency operations. One of their most important current roles is protecting the U.S. skies from further terrorist attacks as part of Operation Noble Eagle.

A three-ship formation of Air National Guard F-16 Flying Falcons.

Fighter aircraft, such as F-15 Eagle, F-16 Fighting Falcon, and YF-22 Raptor jets, are used to defend U.S. troops and citizens against enemy aircraft. USAF fighters are made to be fast, maneuverable, tough, and destructive, and they are mainly armed with air-to-air missiles (AAMs), such as the AIM-9 Sidewinder or the AIM-120 AMRAAM. The role of strike/attack aircraft is to attack enemy ground targets, often in advance of an assault by ground forces. During the Gulf War, for example, U.S. F-111, F-117, and F-15E jets destroyed thousands of Iraqi military vehicles and almost all Iraqi communications and radar systems. As of 2016, the F-111s and F-117s had been retired from use. The F-111s were replaced by the F-15E Strike Eagle, made by Boeing. This aircraft has seen service in Iraq, Afghanistan, and Libya.

The Air Force also uses strategic bombers. These are huge aircraft, such as the B-52 Stratofortress and Rockwell B-1B, and their role is primarily to produce massive bombardments of enemy ground positions or to launch nuclear missiles from the air. Strategic bombers tend to be used only in situations in which there is little or no risk from enemy ground fire, because they are slow aircraft and difficult to maneuver.

A captain and lieutenant in the lower deck of a B-52 Stratofortress.

Combat, however, is only one aspect of USAF duties. Another vital mission is airborne recon-naissance. Aircraft such as the E-3 AWACS, E-8 Joint Stars, RC-135V, and Lockheed U-2R can provide detailed surveillance images of the ground below them from a high altitude, regardless of the weather or battlefield conditions. These images are transmitted to Army, Navy, or Air Force units for tactical use. Surveillance aircraft also perform combat flight-control services, warning USAF aircraft of enemy planes and directing them into the right position to attack.

A similar, but more aggressive, role of USAF aircraft is combat support. Combat support involves aircraft deliberately destroying or jamming enemy communications, radar, or surface-to-air missile (SAM) systems.

By jamming or destroying enemy systems, the combat-support aircraft provide fighters, attack aircraft, and strategic bombers with safer air corridors and greater chances of success-fully completing their missions.

Many USAF aircraft are not involved directly in combat but are still vital to effective air operations. Boeing KC-135 Stratotankers provide in-flight refueling for other U.S. aircraft, giving them the ability to fly to international locations without having to land and refuel. Every year, USAF transport aircraft carry millions of tons of equipment around the world. The real value of military transport aircraft is their speed. Whereas a ship can take up to a week to sail from the United States to the Middle East, transport aircraft, such as the C-5 Galaxy and C-141 Starlifter, can do it in a day, and deliver anything from tanks to troops.

Apart from the roles outlined, USAF aircraft perform a multitude of other duties, including deploying special forces units, flying prominent or important people, training airmen, and even displaying flying techniques at air shows. Each role contributes to making the Air Force capable of tackling any military, peacemaking, or humanitarian mission anywhere in the world.

Text-Dependent Questions

1. What officer of the U.S. Air Force is responsible for Air Force deployments and operations?
2. Which command of the Air Force controls nearly one-third of U.S. nuclear capability?
3. How much territory is the PACAF responsible for?

Research Projects

1. Since its formation in 1997, how many times has the AFRC been deployed? What have been their primary missions?
2. In addition to flying, what are the other jobs personnel perform in the U.S. Air Force? What kind of technology-related jobs are available?

CHAPTER 3

TRAINING FOR COMBAT

The deputy director for requirements greeting a Joint Specialized Undergraduate Pilot Class.

t takes well over a year to create a U.S. Air Force pilot. Many of those who start the training are not there to complete the program at the end of it, but those who do remain stand apart as the elite. Pilot training is one of the most demanding programs of military instruction in the world, and only those with strong bodies and exceptional minds make the grade.

It should be remembered that there are literally hundreds of different careers in the Air Force. Engineers, cooks, radar operators, lawyers, technicians, designers, administrators—the list of different jobs runs on and on. However, the fact remains that the public is initially most interested in what it takes to become a USAF pilot, as this chapter will explain.

Military Boot Camp

Pilots and all other Air Force personnel must undergo the six-week U. S. Air Force Basic Military Training (BT) program held at the 737th Air Force Base (AFB), in San Antonio, TX. More than 35,000 new recruits pass through this program every year. Although a small proportion of these people will go on to become pilots, the six weeks of BT make no distinction between individuals of whatever rank or role.

The first week of BT is mostly spent sorting out administration and processing matters. New recruits are met at San Antonio Airport by their Training Instructors (TIs), who

Words to Understand

Aerodynamics: Science that studies movements in air, including objects moving through air.

Depressurized: Released pressure from.

Simulators: Machines used to show what something is like, usually used to train people.

then take them on a bus to Lackland AFB. The first week involves new recruits being assigned a dormitory, receiving their uniform, having a close haircut, learning basic rules and regulations, and filling in forms. Those who are unfit or overweight are sometimes put on the PT Flight, a program of intense physical exercise to bring them into shape. The recruits receive vaccinations and a dental inspection to make sure that they are fit to train.

Being a Fighter Pilot

Major Fritz Heck, USAF fighter pilot, recalls how he became a pilot and what life is like in the USAF: I got a brochure in the mail when I was a junior at high school for the Air Force Academy. I had always wanted to fly airplanes ever since I was a little kid. I looked at the brochure and thought this looked like a good way to get to where I wanted to be. So, I mailed the application to the Air Force Academy and sent the application to my congressman for review. I then had to have an interview with my congressman, and I was one of the few to get a nomination. Then my dream came true—I was accepted into the Air Force Academy.

I flew combat operations in Operation Northern Watch, Operation Southern Watch, Joint Guard, Deny Flight, Provide Comfort, and Allied Force. It was a very busy time for me, and a combat operation was one of the most exciting things I ever did. Now, I'm a test pilot. Planes come into our base for servicing and maintenance. It's up to me to test them out and really push them to their limits to make sure that they're suitable for flying in combat.

Actual Air Force BT begins the second week. Although the Air Force BT does not have the tough reputation of Marine Corps or Army Rangers training, the initial weeks are surprisingly similar and demanding. The TIs are demanding and critical individuals who spot every mistake and pounce on every sign of inefficiency. The recruits do increasingly tougher physical exercises under the watchful gaze of the TI, and they also learn the basics of saluting, parade-ground drill (known as flight drill), and how to clean and prepare their dormitory for inspection.

Basic training pushes young men and women to their physical limits with various obstacle courses.

On average, they will receive two dormitory inspections per week, and they are harshly punished for any failings. Academic classes also begin. During BT, recruits can expect to do 40 hours of classroom work. Subjects covered include Air Force history, Air Force organization, financial management, customs and courtesies, health and fitness, and human relations (discussing how to work as a team). The TIs expect to see the recruits work as hard in the classroom as they do in the exercise yard.

Air Force basic training (the first 4 weeks.)

In weeks three and four, the recruits are tested on everything they have learned to date. To keep their feet on the ground, they will also be put on Kitchen Patrol, which means helping to

keep the camp kitchens spotlessly clean. Physical training gets harder and harder, but the recruits also acquire basic principles of military operations. Week five is called Warrior Week, and for good reason. For the entire week, the recruits live out in the field in tents, learning survival skills, shooting the Ml6 rifle, and tackling tough military obstacle courses.

They also experience chemical-warfare training. Part of this involves a spell in the "gas chamber," a CS-gas-filled room in which recruits must take off their gas mask twice and recount their name, rank, and social security number. The TIs also give the recruits mental tests and exercises that push their ability to work as a team and show initiative.

After Warrior Week, the final week is spent winding down. Unless the recruits make any serious mistakes in this last week, they will pass through the next level of training. A recruit intent on being a pilot then faces over a year of additional training.

Basic training also includes a lot of time spent in the classroom and studying.

Pilot Training

Flight training takes place at Randolph AFB, TX. There are three main stages. First, the pilot candidates undergo Introductory Flight Training (IFT), in which they receive 50 hours of flying instruction to gain their private pilot license (although many pilot candidates arrive in Randolph having already acquired this license).

After IFT, recruits go in one of two directions. They can attend either the Euro-NATO Joint Jet Pilot Training (ENJJPT) or the Joint Specialized Undergraduate Pilot Training (JSUPT). Both courses are extremely demanding and last around 52–54 weeks. ENJJPT teaches the pilot candidate to fly military jets in association with NATO allies, and some instruction is carried out by European officers. By contrast, JSUPT focuses on USAF flying and aircraft. This book will examine in more detail the processes of JSUPT.

JSUPT usually lasts 52 weeks. At the end, candidates will be fully qualified pilots. There are three phases to training. Phase one lasts for one month and consists mainly of classroom instruction in the basics of military aviation. Academic work is extremely important and highly technical in USAF pilot training. Courses include aerospace physiology, fundamentals of flying, **aerodynamics**, mission planning, navigation, aviation weather, crisis handling, military intelligence, and theoretical training in the aircraft they will fly. All academic work is tested at regular intervals, and the pilot candidates must pass each test to complete the course.

Phase two sees the pilot candidates begin their military flight training. This phase lasts for six months and is normally conducted in T-34, T-37, or T-6 Texan II training aircraft. Phase two teaches the pilot candidates the fundamentals of flying military aircraft. They will spend time in the air and also in flying **simulators** on the ground, and the instructors will test their ability to respond to in-flight crises and problems. In particular, instructors will look to see that candidates can cope with stressful events while suffering from the extreme physical effects of flying a modern jet.

Written exams are administered to pilot candidates through phase one of their training. The written exam tests the candidates' knowledge on weapons loading operations and safety standards.

If the pilot candidates pass all stages of phase two, they will then proceed to one of four advanced training tracks, depending on what type of aircraft they want to fly. These tracks are as follows, alongside the length of training, the training aircraft used, and the training bases:

- **Advanced Fighter: six months; USAF T-38 aircraft; Columbus AFB, Vance AFB, Laughlin AFB**
- **Advanced Tanker/Transport/Bomber: six months; USAF T-I aircraft; Columbus AFB, Vance AFB, Laughlin AFB**
- **Advanced Prop: six months; USN T-44; NAS Corpus Christi**
- **Advanced Helicopter (Army): seven months; various aircraft; Fort Rucker**

The third phase, advanced training, is the most demanding stage for the pilot candidates. They will be tested constantly under high-pressure situations, and both mind and body will be pushed to the very limits of endurance. If they can make it through, however, they will successfully graduate as USAF pilots.

Ironically, this training may be only the beginning. Once they are trained in a particular style of aviation, they must go on to a distinct squadron and train in an individual aircraft, such as the F-15 Eagle or F-16 Falcon (for fighter pilots) or the C-130 Hercules (for transportation pilots).

After bouts of training, pilot candidates will learn to fly aircraft such as the F-15 Eagle (pictured here) or the F-16 Falcon.

Training for the Pressures of Flying

During their pilot training, pilot candidates spend time with the Aerospace Physiology (AP) section. The AP section tests the pilot candidates' ability to cope with the physical strain of flying modern aircraft. One test involves a piece of equipment called the hypobaric altitude chamber. This is a chamber on the ground capable of simulating the low air pressures and reduced oxygen levels a pilot would feel at high altitude if the plane suddenly depressurized.

The pilot candidates sit wearing oxygen masks in the chamber while the pressure is lowered to simulate an altitude of 50,000 ft (16,400 m). Then they are told to remove the masks. As soon as they do so, they start to suffer from the effects of oxygen deprivation to the brain. They feel light-headed, dizzy, nauseous, and find it hard to think straight. For a short period of time, the instructors will try to get them to accomplish mental tasks to see how they cope with the problem. However, they are soon told to put their masks back on—before they lose consciousness. Other tests in the AP section include parachute and ejection-seat training, and also subjecting the pilots to high G-forces to see how well they cope.

An airman undergoing training in the hypobaric altitude chamber, which simulates the low air pressures and reduced oxygen levels a pilot would feel if the plane suddenly lost pressure.

The length of training ensures that those who become USAF pilots are among the elite. Today, no nation on Earth trains its pilots better than the United States does. Indeed, in recent examples of aerial combat, the USAF has almost always come out on top.

Text-Dependent Questions

1. How many weeks is the Air Force basic training program?
2. How many hours of academic training do recruits receive during Basic Training?
3. Introductory Flight Training includes how many hours of flight instruction?

Research Projects

1. Research parachute training. How many Air Force personnel are required to complete it? What does it involve?
2. How many officers are in the Air Force? How many Air Force personnel pursue officer training? What percentage of personnel complete it and go on to become officers?

CHAPTER 4

AIRCRAFT AND TECHNOLOGY

A USAF F-35A Lightning II Joint Strike Fighter leads a formation of other fighter jets near Las Vegas, NV.

The U.S. Air Force has set the world standard for technical excellence in military aviation. Its aircraft possess the ultimate in firepower, speed, and computer technology.

In World War II, a U.S. fighter pilot flying into combat in a P-51 Mustang, for example, had a maximum speed of 437 mph (784 km/h). This speed meant that, if he spotted enemy aircraft in the far distance, he only had a couple of minutes in which to prepare for action. His aircraft was armed with six 0.5-inch (1.27 cm) machine guns, and could also carry two 1,000 lb (454 kg) bombs or six 5-inch (12.7 cm) rockets. At full power, using his Packard Rolls-Royce Merlin V-12 piston engine, he could climb to 30,000 ft (9,145 m) in 13 minutes. Fitted with external fuel tanks, the Mustang had a maximum flying range of 2,080 miles (3,347 km), and it could operate to a maximum height of 41,900 ft (12,770 m). The Mustang was one of the greatest fighter aircraft of the entire war, and few enemy aircraft could match its capabilities.

Now, leap forward 50 years and see how the experience of modern USAF fighter pilots differs from that of their predecessors. In this instance, the pilot is flying a McDonnell Douglas F-15 Eagle, possibly the best all-around fighter aircraft in the world today.

Seeing the enemy in the far distance, the F-15 pilot has only two or three seconds in which to make evasive or combat maneuvers—the Eagle's maximum speed is over 1,650 mph (2,655 km/h). Its two Pratt & Whitney F100-P220 jet engines each produce 14,370 lb (6,518 kg) of thrust, letting it climb at a dizzying 50,000 ft (15,240 m) per minute. The F-15's

Words to Understand

Annihilate: Destroy completely.

Cruise missiles: Low-flying missile guided by an on-board computer.

Depleted-uranium ammunition: Steel-penetrating arrows made of uranium metal.

range can extend to 3,450 miles (5,560 km), and in addition, the aircraft has a practical altitude ceiling of 60,000 ft (18,290 m).

Perhaps the most striking difference between the Mustang and the Eagle lies in armaments. The Eagle is armed with a 20 mm M16A-1 cannon, eight guided air-to-air missiles, and more than 16,000 lb (7,258 kg) of bombs and other missile technologies. Its destructive force is astounding. Using an AIM-120 Advance Medium-Range Air-to-Air Missile (AMRAAM), for example, the Eagle is able to engage and destroy an enemy aircraft over 20 miles (32 km) away, well beyond the visual range of the pilot. Laser-guided bombs, such as the GBU-24 Paveway III, can explode a 2000 lb (907 kg) warhead on target with an accuracy of only a few feet from the aiming point.

Most dramatically, an Eagle can also drop a B61 tactical nuclear bomb, which has an explosive force equivalent to 500,000 tons of dynamite. These weapons are only a selection of those the Eagle can carry, and few who have ever been attacked by such an aircraft can forget the experience, if they survive. This comparison between the Mustang and the Eagle shows how far the USAF has come in only half a century. Today's pilots face the same life-or-death challenges the pilots in World War II faced, but their war machines are infinitely more advanced.

The Eagle is only one of the USAF's fleet of superior aircraft. This chapter will look at the different aircraft that fulfill the USAF's fighter and ground-attack roles. Each of these aircraft types represents the best in its class, and they demonstrate why the USAF is the world's dominant air force.

Fighters

Fighters engage and destroy enemy aircraft in air-to-air combat. Actually, few USAF aircraft are totally dedicated to the fighter role. Most fighter-capable aircraft are designated as "strike fighters," meaning that they perform ground-attack duties as well as air interceptions. However, within the United States itself, the Air National Guard deploys McDonnell Douglas F-15 Eagles and General Dynamics F-16 Fighting Falcons dedicated to domestic air-interception duties. F-15 units are based on the west and east coasts of the United States and on Hawaii to protect from overseas attacks. F-16 units are found across the U.S. landmass, providing internal air defense. Whether serving in the Air National Guard or in the regular Air Force overseas, these two fighters present a formidable barrier to any enemy's attempt to control airspace.

Ultimate Explosives

During the war in Afghanistan in 2002, a fearful weapon was dropped on enemy positions. This was the BLU-82 15,000 lb (6,804 kg) bomb, also known as the Daisy Cutter. Some say it is named after the ground pattern left after deployment seen from above. The BLU-82 was originally developed to create instant landing zones for helicopters in the jungles of Vietnam. It consists of a huge metal case filled with 12,600 lb (5,715 kg) of jellied explosive. The bomb is so big that it has to be mounted on a cargo palette and pushed out the back of an MC-130 transport aircraft. When it hits the ground, the explosion is so big that everything within a diameter of 1,829 ft (600 m) is vaporized. In the Gulf War, 11 such bombs were dropped, mainly to cause psychological damage to the enemy. In Afghanistan, the BLU-82 was used as an "earthquake" bomb to kill Taliban fighters hiding in mountainous cave systems.

The F-16 was developed in the 1970s as a highly maneuverable air-superiority fighter. It can fly at 1,350 mph (2,172 km/h) and is armed with one 20 mm M61 cannon, AMRAAM, Sparrow and Sidewinder AAMs, and a weapons load of 17,200 lb (7,802 kg). This craft is un-usual in that the F-16 pilot does not fly using a central joystick. Instead, the control is a small handle only a few inches high set to the right-hand side of the pilot's seat.

Interestingly, the F-16 is the most commercially successful warplane since World War II. More than 4,000 have been produced, and more than 18 nations use the F-16.

Two new fighters are part of the USAF's Advanced Tactical Fighter program. One is the Lockheed F-22 Raptor, a highly maneuverable, ultra-high-tech fighter that has sophisticated features, such as thrust vectoring (the direction of blast from the jets can be altered to increase maneuverability) and radar-absorbent materials to diminish its appearance on enemy radar. The other is the Lockheed Martin X-35 Joint Strike Fighter (JSF). This aircraft, a joint project between the United States and Canada, began service in 2006. With its Short Takeoff and Landing (STL) ability the jet exhausts can be angled to let the jet take off from, or land on, short landing strips. Although the F-15 and F-16 will continue to serve as fine aircraft for many more years, the Raptor and JSF will keep the USAF at the top of aviation technology.

A Lockheed Martin F-22 Raptor.

Strike Fighters and Attack Aircraft

Wherever it is deployed, the USAF has total air superiority. Consequently, few enemy forces will actually fight the USAF in the air. Those that have recently been tempted to do so, such as Iraq in the Gulf War, were utterly **annihilated**. With few air-to-air combat duties, the USAF is usually employed in attacking ground targets.

Two types of aircraft fulfill this role. One is the strike fighter, a versatile fighter aircraft that is also capable of making ground-attack missions. The other is the attack aircraft, dedicated to pounding enemy land targets.

The USAF has a vast range of strike/attack aircraft. One of its most important is actually a variant of the F-15 Eagle, known as the F-15E. The F-15E has the same performance abilities as the standard fighter version, but it carries more advanced electronics and is also able to support heavier weights of ammunition, bombs, and missiles. F-15Es have been used hard over recent years, bombing targets from the deserts of Iraq to the snow-covered mountains of Afghanistan, and they have always proved themselves to be excellent strike aircraft. By far, however, the most technologically advanced strike fighters are the "stealth fighters"—the F-117 Night Hawk and its successor the F-22 Raptor. The stealth fighters employ what is known as "low observables" technology, also called stealth technology. A special radar-absorbent material is applied to the surface of the aircraft. This material, combined with the slim angular shape of the aircraft, absorbs and deflects enemy radar signals and makes it almost invisible to enemy electronic surveillance. The aircraft also uses special engines that produce little noise, no visible exhaust, and little heat signature. All these capabilities enable the stealth fighters to creep up on enemy targets, cruising at a speed of around 580 mph (933 km/h), before delivering up to 4,000 lb (1,814 kg) of precision-guided, high-explosive bombs. During Operation Desert Storm, F-117 aircraft flew 1,271 combat sorties in 42 days without a single loss—testimony to the superiority of these planes.

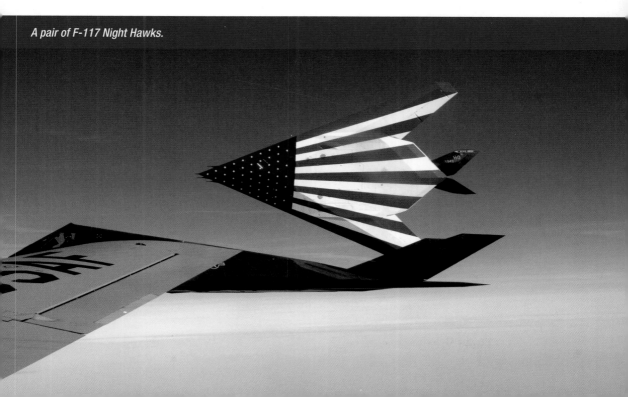

A pair of F-117 Night Hawks.

Not all the USAF's strike aircraft are as sophisticated as the F-117, each of which costs $45 million. Another veteran of the Gulf War is the Fairchild A-10 Thunderbolt II, each costing a much more reasonable $9.8 million. The Thunderbolt is a tank-busting aircraft. It is slow—maximum speed is about 439 mph (706 km/h)—but it is heavily

The history of the stealth fighters.

protected with titanium armor and can carry up to 16,000 lb (7,258 kg) of bombs and AGM-65 Maverick air-to-surface missiles (ASMs). However, its main weapon is the enormous General Electric GAU-8/A Avenger 30 mm seven-barrel cannon. This lethal weapon fires armor-piercing **depleted-uranium ammunition** at either 2,100 or 4,200 rounds per minute. Just a two-second burst from this mighty weapon will destroy the largest main battle tanks. In the Gulf War, Thunderbolts destroyed hundreds of Iraqi vehicles and became one of the USAF's most feared ground-attack weapons.

The USAF's huge inventory of weapons includes many more than the ones listed in this section. Air-launched Tomahawk **cruise missiles** can fly hundreds of miles, hugging the terrain, before hitting a target with pinpoint precision. A Boeing B-52 Stratofortress can annihilate almost a square mile (2.5 sq km) of terrain with up to 50,000 lb (22,680 kg) of bombs in a single pass. The B2 "stealth bomber" has all the stealth properties of the F-117 but is capable of dropping nuclear weapons or 24,000 lb (10,890 kg) of conventional explosives. It is also the most expensive aircraft ever made, each one costing over $1 billion. Such weapons ensure that the USAF can handle any threat or challenge and totally dominate the airspace.

Maintaining and developing such a cutting-edge military force does not come cheap. The current military budget for the U.S. Air Force is around $317 billion.

A B-52 Stratofortress supporting Operation Polar Roar—an operation designed to strengthen cooperation among bomber crews.

Text-Dependent Questions

1. What was the maximum speed of the P-51 Mustang flown in World War II?
2. What role do fighters play in the U.S. Air Force?
3. Which aircraft are capable of performing ground attacks?

Research Projects

1. Research the P-52 Mustang. How many were operational during World War II? How many missions did they fly and how many pilots flew them?
2. Research stealth fighters. What technologies do they come equipped with and what kind of missions do these aircraft typically execute?

CHAPTER 5

SURVEILLANCE AND ELECTRONIC DEFENSE

Pre-flight inspection of an E-8C Joint Surveillance and Target Attack Radar System (STARS) aircraft. Joint STARS provide command and control, intelligence, surveillance, and reconnaissance.

The U.S. Air Force is watching the world 24 hours a day. Surveillance satellites, reconnaissance aircraft, and sophisticated radar provide the United States with an accurate picture of what potentially hostile nations are doing.

Accurate surveillance is vital for all military operations. One of the best examples of this occurred in the Gulf War (1990–1991). At the beginning of the war, the biggest threat to U.S. and Allied aircraft was Iraq's extensive radar system. Iraq had a massive system of surface-to-air missiles (SAMs), each missile controlled by a network of targeting radars threaded throughout Iraq and occupied Kuwait. If the Allies were to achieve air superiority, this radar system had to be taken out.

To accomplish this, USAF Grumman/General Dynamics EF-111A Ravens and U.S. Navy/Marine Corps Grumman EA-6B Prowlers flew surveillance missions over Iraq and plotted almost all enemy radar systems. One particularly clever technique used by the USAF was to send large flights of jets toward the Iraqi border, prompting the SAM operators to turn on all their radar systems. As soon as they were turned on, the U.S. jets turned around and flew back to safety, while the surveillance aircraft quickly plotted every single SAM position by using the targeting signals. Once a full picture of Iraqi command-and-control systems had been created, U.S. and British warplanes flew in and fired antiradar missiles to wipe out the targets. Those Iraqi radar positions that were not destroyed had their signals jammed by USAF Lockheed EC-130H Compass Call aircraft, which carry the ALQ-99 Tactical Jamming

Words to Understand

Consoles: Cabinets that stand on the floor.

Fuselage: The central portion of an aircraft that accommodates passengers or cargo.

G-force: The force of of gravity or acceleration on a body.

System on board. Iraq found itself completely blind, unable to monitor or detect enemy forces. By contrast, the USAF was able to watch Iraqi ground and air forces around the clock.

Surveillance Technologies

The USAF has three main types of surveillance technology: airborne surveillance, ground-based radar, and satellite surveillance. This chapter will examine airborne surveillance—satellite and radar surveillance is described in the next chapter.

The U-2 Incident

In the 1950s, the USAF's main high-altitude surveillance aircraft was the U-2. This amazing aircraft could fly at an altitude of 75,000 ft (24,600 m). Even at that altitude, its onboard cameras were capable of photographing a golf ball on a putting green. Between 1955 and 1960, U-2s conducted regular surveillance missions over the Soviet Union, high above enemy surface-to-air missiles (SAMs). However, in the late 1950s, the Soviet Union acquired the high-altitude SAM-2 weapon, and on May 1, 1960, a U-2 flown by USAF pilot Gary Powers was shot down. The United States faced a delicate situation. Powers was captured, but President Eisenhower initially denied that the aircraft was flying in Soviet airspace. Then on May 7, 1960, the Soviet leader Khrushchev announced to the world what had happened and that Powers had been captured. There followed many weeks of difficult negotiations. The Soviets argued that the United States was jeopardizing any chances of peace, while the United States defended itself by saying that it needed to patrol Soviet skies to guard against a surprise attack with nuclear weapons. After the U-2 incident, the United States stopped flying high-altitude missions over the Soviet Union.

Pilot Gary Powers during a hearing on the U-2 Incident in front of a Senate Armed Services Select Committee.

The U.S. Air Force has the most advanced aerial surveillance vehicles in the world. They serve four main purposes: gathering intelligence and surveillance; assisting communications between military units; providing countermeasures against enemy radar and intelligence; and assisting in defining targets for Army, Navy, or Air Force weaponry. Two exceptional aircraft in particular are used in almost every conflict or peacekeeping mission of U.S. forces: the E-3 Sentry Airborne Warning and Control System (AWACS) and the E-8C Joint STARS. Each performs distinct roles, and together they give U.S. forces an eagle-eye view of the battlefield.

E-3 Sentry AWACS aircraft have been used constantly since the early 1990s, and 31 of these aircraft were in use by the Air Force as of September 2015. During Operation Desert Shield in the Gulf War, E-3s flew 24 hours a day, giving Allied aircraft the information needed to fly 120,000 sorties and destroy 38 Iraqi aircraft in the air. The E-3 is actually a converted civil airliner, the Boeing 707. The most striking feature of the conversion is a massive radar dome stuck on top of the **fuselage** —30 ft (9.1 m) in diameter, 6 ft (1.8 m) thick, and supported 14 ft (4.2 m) above the fuselage. This radar is a probing, long-range surveillance instrument. It can scan for enemy ships, vehicles, and aircraft out to a distance of more than 250 miles (375.5 km) and from an altitude of over 9 miles (15 km). The radar has another feature, called identification friend or foe (IFF), which automatically tells the crew if the object detected on the radar is allied or enemy.

Inside the E-3 are banks of computer **consoles** manned by up to 19 specialist communication officers (there are also four flight crew). All information gathered from the radar and other sources is presented on these computers. The information is then transferred to allied command-and-control systems on the ground and in the air via a Joint Tactical Information Distribution System (JTIDS), which is secure from enemy attempts to hack into allied communications. In addition to surveillance, the E-3 is also fitted with Global Positioning System (GPS) technology, which lets it give the exact coordinates of enemy forces to allied troops. All this technology is expensive, however—each Sentry aircraft costs an enormous $123.4 million.

An E-3 Sentry airborne warning and control system aircraft.

While the E-3 Sentry conducts surveillance of land, sea, and air, the E-8C Joint Surveillance Targets Attack Radar System (Joint STARS) is focused on detecting enemy armor on the ground. The E-8C, like the E-3, was developed during the 1980s and first deployed in the Gulf War. During its early operations, E-8Cs detected, monitored, and plotted hundreds of Iraqi tanks and mobile missile launches, most of which were then destroyed by allied strike-aircraft using the E-8C's information.

Again, the E-8C is a modified Boeing 707, but unlike the E-3, its main radar is housed in a 40 ft (12 m) long tube attached beneath the fuselage. This radar can detect vehicles moving within an area of 19,305 square miles (50,000 sq km), and track multiple targets simultaneously. Its moving target indicator (MTI) and fixed target indicator (FTI) can distinguish between static and mobile targets, and this information is relayed in "real time" to Army ground stations. "Real time" surveillance means that the information is updated almost every second. E-8Cs can control attacks from infantry, artillery, naval gunfire, and attack aircraft, and in the Gulf War, it had a 100 percent success rate in detecting enemy vehicles and facilitating their destruction. Each E-8C costs a huge $244.4 million and carries four flight crew and 18 onboard specialists.

Unmanned Aerial Vehicles

The Air Force currently has entire squadrons of aircraft with one unusual feature—they have no pilots. These aircraft are known as Unmanned Aerial Vehicles (UAVs), and they may represent the future of air warfare and surveillance. UAVs are aircraft that are flown not by a pilot who sits

Air Force pilots flying MQ-1 Predator drones.

on board but by a controller who stays on the ground and flies the aircraft by remote control. Information from the UAV's onboard cameras and sensors is fed back to the controller, providing all the information needed to fly the aircraft successfully and respond to any unexpected events. UAVs have some amazing advantages over piloted aircraft. They are over 50 percent cheaper to build than piloted aircraft; they can make maneuvers that would render a human pilot unconscious through the effects of **g-force**; training its controller is far quicker; no personnel are put at risk; and they can fly for hours on end, avoiding the problem of a pilot getting tired or needing to land.

This last virtue has made them ideal for use as surveillance aircraft. One of the most important UAVs currently in service is the MQ-1B Predator. A fully operational MQ-1B system consists of four sensor/weapon-equipped aircraft, ground control station, Predator Primary Satellite Link, and spare equipment. It can be deployed for worldwide operations. It can also be disassembled and loaded into a container for travel. The Predator can operate on a 5,000 by 75-foot hard-surface runway with a clear line of sight.

An MQ-1B Predator was used for an unmanned flight during an Operation Iraqi Freedom combat mission. It provided intelligence, search, and reconnaissance gathering features.

This captain and airman act as pilot and sensor operator, handling the MQ-1 Predator, an unmanned aerial vehicle from a control room.

The MQ-1 Predator—an unmanned aircraft—in flight.

Electronic Defense in the Gulf War

Electronic intelligence (ELINT) and aerial surveillance were vital in winning the Gulf War. Equally vital were the efforts of the USAF to degrade and diminish the Iraqi forces' powers of communication. The USAF EC-130H Compass Call aircraft is an airborne tactical weapon system that disrupts enemy command and control communications and limits adversary coordination essential for enemy force management. Over its 32-year operational life, the aircraft has demonstrated a powerful effect on enemy command and control networks in many military operations, including Kosovo, Haiti, Panama, Libya, Iraq, Serbia, and Afghanistan. From 2005 through 2015, it provided crucial support to numerous combat commands, including more than than 26,000 hours of electronic attack for Operation Iraqi Freedom.

With only nine such communications-jamming aircraft during the Gulf War (the Air Force now has 14 of these aircraft), the USAF seriously affected the operational ability of Iraq's military forces. Flying almost 24 hours a day, the EC-130Hs monitored Iraqi airwaves until they picked up communications between enemy units. They then had two options—either record the message for analysis by allied intelligence, or jam the communications. The jamming programs had an instant effect. Iraqi radio operators found their headphones filled with screeching and wailing sounds, and were unable to get rid of them. This disrupted Iraqi communications and so reduced their military effectiveness. In addition, Compass Call flights sometimes carried Iraqi-speaking operators on board, who would relay fake commands to enemy units, leading them into ambushes or air strikes. The efforts of Compass Call flights, and the quick responses of Allied attack aircraft, meant that in only six days, Iraqi surface-to-air missile (SAM) batteries suffered a 95 percent reduction in activity.

The other main UAV is the Global Hawk. This is a larger vehicle than the Predator, but it has a range of over 13,800 miles (22,208 km) and can fly at altitudes of up to 65,000 ft (19,812 m). Using the sophisticated Synthetic Aperture Radar/Ground Moving Target Indicator, it can plot every target in an area the size of Illinois (46,000 sq m/119,094 km) in only 24 hours.

It can remain flying over the battlefield (known as being "in station") for 24 hours—and this after flying a distance of up to 1,200 miles (1,931 km) to the surveillance area. Global Hawk is also being armed, and the future of aerial warfare seems deeply involved with the development of UAVs.

Text-Dependent Questions

1. What is the primary difference between surveillance aircraft and fighters?
2. How are E-3 Sentry aircraft controlled?
3. What is the main function of the Compass Call?

Research Projects

1. What training do Air Force personnel need to fly unmanned aircraft? Is a pilot license required? Is there additional special training?
2. What role have unmanned aircraft played in the war against ISIS? How often have they been used and for what purpose?

CHAPTER 6

THE U.S. AIR FORCE IN SPACE

A United Launch Delta IV Medium launches from Vandenberg Air Force Base.

The U.S. Air Force is active hundreds of miles above Earth's surface. Its Air Force Space Command explores the opportunities that space presents for the defensive and offensive capabilities of the United States.

Air Force Space Command (AFSPC) was created on September 1, 1982. It is possibly the most powerful command of any branch of the U.S. military because it maintains and operates all U.S. nuclear **intercontinental** ballistic missiles (ICBMs). Day and night, it monitors the entire world and acts as a real deterrent to aggressive nations possibly using nuclear weapons against the United States.

AFSPC has many other duties besides operating its nuclear arsenal. It launches military and navigational satellites into space. It monitors space itself, plotting the positions and behavior of non-U.S. space vehicles and potentially dangerous space debris. Its satellite systems provide weather information, worldwide communications, missile warnings, and navigational systems to soldiers on the ground. With over 33,000 people employed in these roles, AFSPC is a vital organization for U.S. defense.

Nuclear Force and Detection

U.S. ICBM defenses are effectively run by two units: the 14th Air Force, based at Vandenberg Air Force Base (AFB), CA, and the 90th Space Wing at Warren AFB, WY. The 14th Air Force controls a network of Defense Support Program (DSP) satellites, which monitor Earth from a

Words to Understand

Coordinates: Set of numbers used to locate a point on a map.

Infrared: Light rays that can't be seen and that are longer than rays that produce red light.

Intercontinental: Capable of traveling from one continent to another.

distance of 22,000 miles (35,404 km), using **infrared** detectors to look for any sign of missile launches. Each DSP satellite contains over 2,000 detectors, and all data they receive is passed on to North American Air Defense Command (NORAD) and United States Space Command (USSPACECOM) early-warning centers at Cheyenne Mountain, CO, and to National Command Authorities. The 90th Space Wing is responsible for operating U.S. ICBM weapon systems themselves, such as the Minuteman and Peacemaker missiles. It is an elite unit, and remains in a state of over 99 percent readiness—which simply means that it is always prepared to respond within minutes to any nuclear threat. U.S. nuclear forces have maintained a 24-hour alert since 1959. The United States currently has 450 ICBMs in its weaponry. All of them are contained in reinforced-concrete launch silos situated beneath the Great Plains.

Air Force Space Command headquarters.

DSP satellites are eventually to be surpassed by the Space-Based Infrared System (SBIRS) system. The SBIRS will contain around 30 satellites to give extremely precise coordinates of any missile launch, a faster report time to commanders back in the United States, and more accurate prediction of where the missile will land. But satellites are not the only systems of monitoring the world for missile launches. The USAF also operates a network of ground-based early-warning radars in the United States and abroad. The most sophisticated of these is the PAVE PAWS (Phased Array Warning System—"PAVE" is a military program identification code) radar system, which not only tracks earth-orbiting satellites but can also simultaneously detect and monitor hundreds of missiles if they are launched.

To defend against such an attack, the USAF is developing laser-defense systems. These are powerful laser weapons that will be deployed in orbiting satellites to destroy enemy ICBMs as they fly through space and Earth's atmosphere. Based on current Space-Based Laser (SBL) technology, the time from detection of a missile to its destruction would be only 1–10 seconds.

The Cuban Missile Crisis

In 1962, the world came the closest it has ever been to nuclear war. The United States and the Soviet Union were locked in a nuclear arms race, and the Soviets were losing. Although U.S. missiles could easily reach the Soviet Union, Communist nuclear weapons could reach only as far as Europe. The Soviet solution was to construct nuclear-missile launch facilities on the Communist island of Cuba, only about a hundred miles from the U.S. coast. On October 15, 1962, President John F. Kennedy was informed of this construction—and he took swift action.

A ring of Navy ships and USAF aircraft surrounded Cuba, stopping Soviet ships from bringing in more missiles. Kennedy also demanded the removal of all existing missiles. Tensions began to build as Soviet and U.S. Navy ships faced each other, preparing for battle. On October 27, a U-2 reconnaissance aircraft was shot down over Cuba, and for 24 hours, the world feared it would be plunged into nuclear war. At the last minute, President Kennedy and the Soviet leader, Nikita Khrushchev, reached an agreement. The Soviet Union agreed to remove its missiles from Cuba, and the United States promised not to invade the island. The entire world breathed a sigh of relief.

Satellite and Surveillance Support

The AFSPC is not just concerned with nuclear defense. It also deploys, operates, and monitors a range of satellite services, without which the U.S. military would be severely weakened. Possibly the most important is Navstar, or the Global Positioning System (GPS). GPS consists of 24 satellites, each of which orbits Earth every 12 hours, emitting continuous navigation signals. Military and civilian personnel on the ground use a special receiver to receive these signals and determine their exact **coordinates** to an accuracy of within 100 ft (33 m). GPS is now essential for military operations. Army, Navy, and Air Force navigators rely on GPS to plot their positions, and many precision-guided missiles and bombs now use GPS to guide them to their targets.

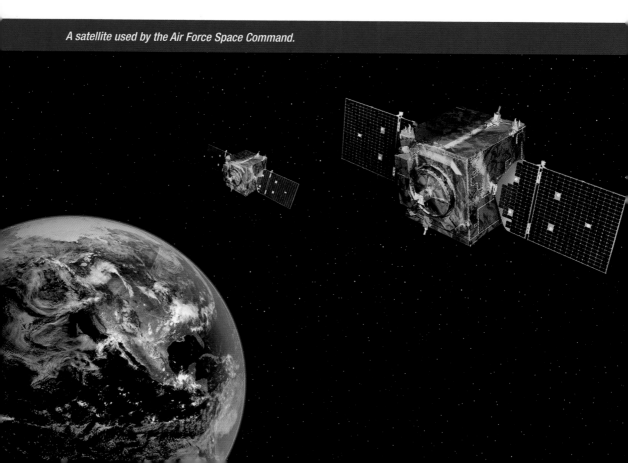

A satellite used by the Air Force Space Command.

In addition to GPS, AFSPC serves the military community by providing the Defense Satellite Communications System (DSCS). Ten Phase III DSCS satellites orbit Earth at an altitude of 23,000 miles (37,013 km). They provide secure worldwide communications for all U.S. military forces, and they are totally resistant to any attempts to jam them. The DSCS satellites are also part of the U.S. early-warning system, and every day, confidential information flits around the world at lightning speed. Another more advanced communications system is the Milstar, which is described as a "smart switchboard." The Milstar not only enables voice communications but can also transfer encrypted voice, data, Teletype, or facsimile communications safe from prying eyes.

Not all frontline AFSPC technology is based in space. One important role based on land is the Ground-Based Electro-Optical Deep Space Surveillance (GEODSS) system, which has its headquarters in the U.S. Space Command's Space Control Center in Cheyenne Mountain Air Force Station, Colorado Springs, CO. Using a mixture of telescopes, low-light-level television cameras, radars, and advanced computers, GEODSS tracks some of the more than 10,000 objects that orbit Earth. Most of these objects are humanmade, such as satellites or pieces of debris from space vehicles that have broken up, but GEODSS also tracks potentially hazardous meteors and comets. The GEODSS telescopes are so sensitive that they can monitor objects 10,000 times dimmer than the dimmest object visible to the human eye. By tracking such objects, GEODSS is able to protect the United States from space objects suddenly entering Earth's atmosphere.

The Ground-Based Electro-Optical Deep Space Surveillance facility at Detachment 2, in Diego Garcia, British Indian Ocean Territory is one of three operational sites worldwide.

Text-Dependent Questions

1. When was the Air Force Space Command created?
2. Which two units run U.S. ICBM defenses?
3. Name the capabilities of the PAVE PAWS radar system.

Research Projects

1. What objects has GEODSS tracked over the past year? Once it spots something potentially dangerous, what is the next step in protecting the United States?
2. How many Air Force personnel work at NORAD? What is the facility like and what kind of security clearance is necessary to visit and/or work there?

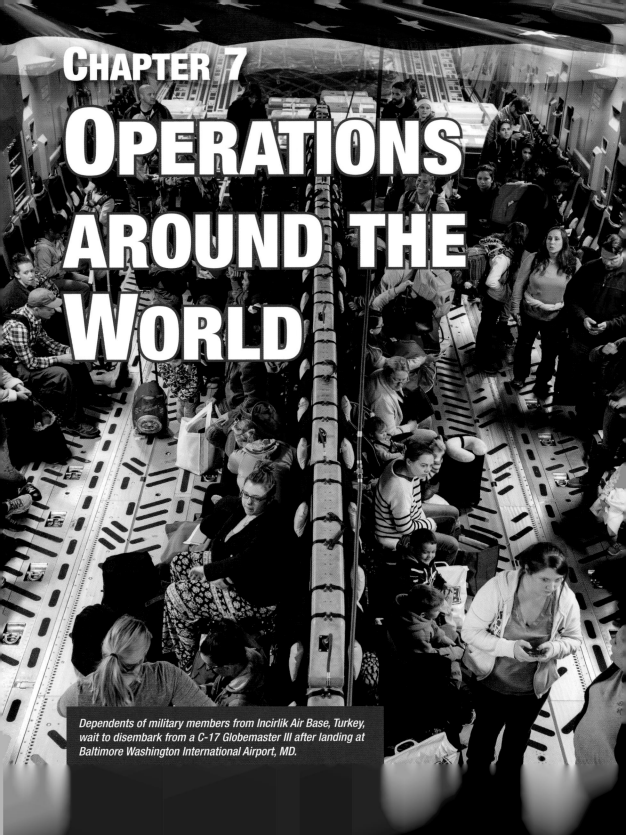

Chapter 7
OPERATIONS AROUND THE WORLD

Dependents of military members from Incirlik Air Base, Turkey, wait to disembark from a C-17 Globemaster III after landing at Baltimore Washington International Airport, MD.

Within a year of its formation, the USAF was performing its first major operation—airlifting supplies into Berlin, West Germany, in defiance of the Communist blockade around the city.

At the end of World War II, Germany was split into two halves. The United States and the Allies controlled the western half; the eastern half was under the jurisdiction of the Communist Soviet Union. Although Germany's capital, Berlin, was set in the Russian sector, the city itself was divided into two halves controlled by the opposing sides. Russia and the United States had been allies during the war, but the end of the war emphasized the differences in their **ideology** and politics, and the former allies became committed enemies.

In June 1948, the Soviets suddenly announced that they were closing U.S. road and rail access routes to Berlin, thereby effectively placing the entire city under Communist control. The United States was faced with a choice: either abandon the city to the Soviets or attempt to use three air corridors to supply West Berlin with all the essentials of living. They chose the second option, and the USAF was called into action.

Citizens of Berlin watch as a Douglas C-54 Skymaster lands at Tempelhof Airport in 1948.

Words to Understand

Humanitarian: Person or organization that works to make others' lives better.

Ideology: Set of ideas or beliefs held by a specific group or political party.

Regime: Form of government or system of management.

The airlift was known as Operation Vittles, and was one of the biggest rescue operations in history. On June 26, 1948, USAF C-47 Dakota aircraft flew 80 tons of supplies into Berlin's Tempelhof Airport. Eighty tons only scratched the surface of what was actually needed, but soon more USAF aircraft and airplanes from the U.S. Navy and British Royal Air Force were helping out. Meanwhile, three USAF bomber groups were sent into the area to provide nuclear deterrence against the Soviets.

Soon, the airlift had reached the stage of landing one aircraft every three minutes, bringing in the 4,500 tons of food, fuel, and other necessities that kept West Berlin alive. There were many dangers, however. Although the Communists did not fire on any of the aircraft, they harassed them by shining intense searchlights at them, jamming their radio communications, and "buzzing" them with fighter aircraft. Because of these efforts, and the dangers of such crowded airspace, 31 U.S. personnel and 34 Allied personnel were killed during the 11-month airlift. Their heroic missions, however, stopped half a city from starving, and on May 12, 1949, the Soviets finally backed down, reopening U.S. and British land routes into the city.

The Berlin airlift was the USAF's first major operation, but it showed the world how significant U.S. military aviation had become. Since World War II, there have been few years in which the USAF has not been involved with major military or **humanitarian** missions. Between 1945 and the mid-1980s, most of these operations were in the context of the Cold War. In the Korean War (1950–1953) and the Vietnam War (1963–1975), USAF units were deployed in force to fight major conflicts and attempt to stop the spread of Communism in the Far East. Since the 1980s, USAF operations have been more concerned with fighting terrorism, controlling aggressive **regimes**, and performing hundreds of rescue and emergency airlifts. This chapter will look at two major conflicts in which the USAF made its presence felt: the Vietnam War and the Persian Gulf War.

The Vietnam War (1963–1975)

Actual fighting between North Vietnam and the United States did not begin until 1964, but the United States had been involved in protecting South Vietnam from Communist takeover since the 1950s. In 1961, USAF and U.S. Army personnel were deployed in South Vietnam to train South

Vietnamese military forces to resist the Communist guerrillas. The USAF was there just to advise, but it was still dangerous work. Soon, four U.S. Army helicopters had been shot down by the Viet Cong, and USAF aircraft were also targeted. Between 1962 and 1964, the USAF gradually played a more active role. Transport aircraft dropped flares over the Vietnamese jungles to expose enemy units, and surveillance aircraft conducted reconnaissance on behalf of the South Vietnamese Army.

Everything changed on August 2, 1964. North Vietnamese torpedo boats attacked the USS *Maddox* floating in the South China Sea, and further attacks against U.S. shipping occurred over the next two nights. In response, President Lyndon B. Johnson authorized the use of air strikes against North Vietnam in retaliation. It was the beginning of the air war.

During 1964, most USAF and U.S. Navy air strikes were in retaliation to attacks on U.S. personnel or installations. However, in 1965, U.S. combat troops were officially deployed in South Vietnam, and the USAF unleashed its full power in Operation Rolling Thunder. Rolling Thunder ran from February 1965 until October 1968, and was one of the heaviest bombing campaigns in history. The operation involved a sustained bombing of North Vietnam, with the intention of forcing them to give up their military action in South Vietnam. Over three years, USAF, U.S. Navy, and U.S. Marine Corps aircraft dropped over one million tons of bombs on North Vietnam.

The main USAF aircraft used in Rolling Thunder were McDonnell Douglas F-4 Phantoms, Republic F-105 Thunderchiefs, North American F-100 Super Sabers, and Douglas A-4 Sky-hawks. All were excellent ground-attack aircraft, and they were put to work demolishing key targets in North Vietnam. These targets included bridges, roads, railroad depots, oil-storage tanks, steelworks, airfields, military bases, communications centers, vital roads, and North Vietnamese supply routes into South Vietnam. Initially, they faced only unsophisticated North Vietnamese machine guns and antiaircraft guns. By 1967, however, North Vietnam had received huge numbers of the modern Soviet SA-2 Guideline surface-to-air missiles (SAMs), which were radar-guided and could hit aircraft at up to 69,000 ft (21,000 m). U.S. pilots often faced a new missile attack every few seconds and had to maneuver their aircraft crazily to shake off the supersonic missiles.

Rolling Thunder was a massive bombardment, but it did not have its intended effect. Although 52,000 North Vietnamese were killed, the bombing did not stop supplies from getting through to the North Vietnamese in South Vietnam. So on October 31, 1968, President Johnson ordered the operation to stop.

Interview with a Vietnam veteran about Operation Rolling Thunder.

USAF operations continued after Rolling Thunder. The Air Force was used mainly to attack Communist units operating in the South Vietnamese jungles and Communist supply routes into South Vietnam through neighboring Laos.

In 1973, all U.S. combat troops on the ground were withdrawn from Vietnam, but the USAF remained to assist South Vietnamese operations until 1975. They were unable to stop the tide of Communism from flooding into South Vietnam, but they did gain huge amounts of combat experience and had demonstrated the power of their technology.

The defeat in Vietnam left all U.S. military forces hugely demoralized. However, in 1990, an operation began that, in the words of President George Bush Sr., "laid to rest the ghosts of Vietnam."

Air Force F-105 Thunderchief pilots bomb a military target in North Vietnam.

Gulf War (1990–1991)

On August 2, 1990, the military forces of Iraq invaded and occupied neighboring Kuwait. This action set alarm bells ringing around the world. Kuwait and its neighbor, Saudi Arabia, were important oil-producing nations, and it looked as if Iraq, led by President Saddam Hussein, was eyeing Saudi Arabia as the next conquest. In response, the United States led a coalition of military forces that were sent to Saudi Arabia as part of Operation Desert Shield. Their mission was to protect Saudi Arabia at all costs.

> ## USAF Combat Controllers
>
> Combat controllers are the unseen warriors of the U.S. Air Force. Their job is to penetrate deep behind enemy lines and pick out targets for destruction by USAF attack aircraft, to conduct rescue operations for downed U.S. pilots, and to act as on-the-ground air traffic controllers for U.S. aircraft. Only 350 combat controllers are qualified, and their training standards are as high as, if not higher than, any elite force in the Army or Navy. They are fully trained in combat, surveillance, covert operations, rescue, combat medicine, and airborne and amphibious deployments, as well as a whole range of other skills. Basic training lasts up to a year, and a typical training exercise involves a three-mile (4.8 km) run followed by a 4,573 ft (1,500 m) swim in uniform. Like the U.S. Navy SEALs, the USAF combat controllers can operate on land, sea, and in the air, and this elite force has been behind the success of many recent USAF missions.

The USAF responded with lightning speed. Only five days after the initial invasion of Kuwait, F-15C Eagle strike-aircraft from the 1st Tactical Fighter Wing, Langley Air Force Base (AFB), VA, landed in Saudi Arabia, and they began flying defensive missions along the Iraqi border only three days later. By January 1991, more than 2,000 U.S. aircraft had been moved into the region. While Desert Shield was in place, Iraq was given an ultimatum: withdraw from Kuwait or face the full might of U.S. and Allied military forces. Saddam Hussein did not respond, and on January 17, 1991, Operation Desert Shield was replaced by Operation Desert Storm.

Once the decision to fight had been made, the USAF and other air forces set to work devastating the Iraqi war machine, one of the most powerful in the Middle East. The first aircraft into action were B-52G Stratofortresses, flying from Barksdale AFB in the United States, and F-117 Stealth fighters. The B-52s fired AGM-86C air-launched cruise missiles at key targets

A Tactical Fighter Wing F-117A stealth fighter aircraft en route to Saudi Arabia during Operation Desert Shield.

within Iraq, while the F-117s flew inside Iraq and smashed radar, air defenses, and communications systems. Soon, the full might of the USAF was brought to bear against the Iraqi forces. Iraqi troops and military vehicles inside Iraq and Kuwait were undoubtedly the hardest hit. Night and day, USAF aircraft pounded troop positions with B-52 bombers or strike aircraft, using precision-guided munitions to wreck tanks, trucks, missile launchers, and other tools of transportation. In addition, Iraq's radar and communications system was almost entirely destroyed. The results of this horrific onslaught were evident when on February 24, 1991, Allied ground forces invaded Kuwait to expel the Iraqi occupiers. They won the battle in only 100 hours. They were able to do so because USAF and Allied airpower had destroyed 60 percent of Iraqi tanks, 40 percent of other armored vehicles, and 60 percent of its artillery. The Iraqi air force lost 234 airplanes. In total, the USAF lost only 13 aircraft.

USAF operations continue to this day over Iraq. Operations Southern Watch and Northern Watch are in force to stop Iraqi aircraft from flying over southern and northern Iraq and threat-

F-16 Falcons prepare to have their weapons armed at Prince Sultan Air Base, Saudi Arabia, during Operation Southern Watch.

ening their neighbors. F-15 and F-16 jets have had to engage Iraqi SAM batteries on many occasions, and the missions over Iraq remain dangerous ones for the USAF.

Since the Gulf War, the USAF has rarely been out of action. In 1992, civil war broke out in Yugoslavia, as the country fragmented into different ethnic and geographical groups. Sarajevo, the capital of Bosnia-Herzegovina (a territory within Yugoslavia), was completely under siege from Bosnians allied with neighboring Serbia. The city was pounded by artillery, and food was running out. In Operation Provide Promise, the USAF flew essential humanitarian supplies into the city. The operation lasted for three and a half years, one of the longest airlift operations in history.

Serbia tried to stop the rescue mission with all their means. USAF aircraft were fired upon, and an Italian transport aircraft was shot down and its crew killed. In response, the USAF and NATO allies began a month-long bombing campaign against Serbia in August 1995. The Serbian capital, Belgrade, and most of its utilities and industry were bombed, the intention being to get the population to put pressure on the government to stop the war. It worked. On November 1, 1995, peace talks began, and these led to a stoppage of aggressive military actions by Serbia and other regions.

Unfortunately, violence flared up again in the region in 1998, this time in the country of Kosovo. Kosovan Serbians and Serbian military forces began to expel or murder ethnic Albanian civilians from the country—Kosovo's population is made up of many people formerly from neighboring Albania. Over 800,000 refugees poured over the border into Albania. Once again, the USAF under NATO command was called into action. U.S. strike-aircraft hunted down Serbian vehicles and troops and bombed them on the ground, while other aircraft hit Belgrade with cruise missiles and precision-guided munitions. Again, the bombing worked, and eventually Serbian forces withdrew from Kosovo.

Operation Enduring Freedom, the war against terrorism that is the response to attacks against the United States, began on September 11, 2001, and ended in 2014. USAF bombing missions used B-52 and B-1 bombers to devastate Taliban fighting positions in Afghanistan. Other Taliban and Al Qaeda soldiers holding out in the mountains suffered tremendous losses from U.S. C-130 aircraft deploying 15,000 lb (6,804 kg) BLU-82 blast bombs. The war against terrorism is far from over, and the Air Force is now involved in the Intervention against the Islamic State of Iraq and the Levant that began in 2014 and continues in 2016. The Air Force has led many aerial attacks during this operation, mainly in Syria and Iraq.

Text-Dependent Questions
1. What was Operation Vittles?
2. What was the Air Force's initial role in the Vietnam War?
3. What did the Air Force do during Operation Provide Promise?

Research Projects
1. Research the U.S. Air Force's role during Operation Enduring Freedom. How many missions were flown and what were their results?
2. Research the F-15C Eagle strike-aircraft. How many are in operation today and what role have they played in recent combat missions?

Series Glosssary

Air marshal: Armed guard traveling on an aircraft to protect the passengers and crew; the air marshal is often disguised as a passenger.

Annexation: To incorporate a country or other territory within the domain of a state.

Armory: A supply of arms for defense or attack.

Assassinate: To murder by sudden or secret attack, usually for impersonal reasons.

Ballistic: Of or relating to firearms.

Biological warfare: Also known as germ warfare, this is war fought with biotoxins—harmful bacteria or viruses that are artificially propagated and deliberately dispersed to spread sickness among an enemy.

Cartel: A combination of groups with a common action or goal.

Chemical warfare: The use of poisonous or corrosive substances to kill or incapacitate the enemy; it differs from biological warfare in that the chemicals concerned are not organic, living germs.

Cold War: A long and bitter enmity between the United States and the Free World and the Soviet Union and its Communist satellites, which went on from 1945 to the collapse of Communism in 1989.

Communism: A system of government in which a single authoritarian party controls state-owned means of production.

Conscription: Compulsory enrollment of persons especially for military service.

Consignment: A shipment of goods or weapons.

Contingency operations: Operations of a short duration and most often performed at short notice, such as dropping supplies into a combat zone.

Counterintelligence: Activities designed to collect information about enemy espionage and then to thwart it.

Covert operations: Secret plans and activities carried out by spies and their agencies.

Cyberterrorism: A form of terrorism that seeks to cause disruption by interfering with computer networks.

Democracy: A government elected to rule by the majority of a country's people.

Depleted uranium: One of the hardest known substances, it has most of its radioactivity removed before being used to make bullets.

Dissident: A person who disagrees with an established religious or political system, organization, or belief.

Embargo: A legal prohibition on commerce.

Emigration: To leave one country to move to another country.

Extortion: The act of obtaining money or other property from a person by means of force or intimidation.

Extradite: To surrender an alleged criminal from one state or nation to another having jurisdiction to try the charge.

Federalize/federalization: The process by which National Guard units, under state command in normal circumstances, are called up by the president in times of crisis to serve the federal government of the United States as a whole.

Genocide: The deliberate and systematic destruction of a racial, political, or cultural group.

Guerrilla: A person who engages in irregular warfare, especially as a member of an independent unit carrying out harassment and sabotage.

Hijack: To take unlawful control of a ship, train, aircraft, or other form of transport.

Immigration: The movement of a person or people ("immigrants") into a country; as opposed to emigration, their movement out.

Indict: To charge with a crime by the finding or presentment of a jury (as a grand jury) in due form of law.

Infiltrate: To penetrate an organization, like a terrorist network.

Infrastructure: The crucial networks of a nation, such as transportation and communication, and also including government organizations, factories, and schools.

Insertion: Getting into a place where hostages are being held.

Insurgent: A person who revolts against civil authority or an established government.

Internment: To hold someone, especially an immigrant, while his or her application for residence is being processed.

Logistics: The aspect of military science dealing with the procurement, maintenance, and transportation of military matériel, facilities, and personnel.

Matériel: Equipment, apparatus, and supplies used by an organization or institution.

Militant: Having a combative or aggressive attitude.

Militia: a military force raised from civilians, which supports a regular army in times of war.

Narcoterrorism: Outrages arranged by drug trafficking gangs to destabilize government, thus weakening law enforcement and creating conditions for the conduct of their illegal business.

NATO: North Atlantic Treaty Organization; an organization of North American and European countries formed in 1949 to protect one another against possible Soviet aggression.

Naturalization: The process by which a foreigner is officially "naturalized," or accepted as a U.S. citizen.

Nonstate actor: A terrorist who does not have official government support.

Ordnance: Military supplies, including weapons, ammunition, combat vehicles, and maintenance tools and equipment.

Refugee: A person forced to take refuge in a country not his or her own, displaced by war or political instability at home.

Rogue state: A country, such as Iraq or North Korea, that ignores the conventions and laws set by the international community; rogue states often pose a threat, either through direct military action or by harboring terrorists.

Sortie: One mission or attack by a single plane.

Sting: A plan implemented by undercover police in order to trap criminals.

Surveillance: To closely watch over and monitor situations; the USAF employs many different kinds of surveillance equipment and techniques in its role as an intelligence gatherer.

Truce: A suspension of fighting by agreement of opposing forces.

UN: United Nations; an international organization, of which the United States is a member, that was established in 1945 to promote international peace and security.

Chronology

1903: The Wright brothers make the world's first flight in a powered, heavier-than-air aircraft.

1907: August 1, U.S. Army Signal Corps forms an Aeronautical Division.

1913: The U.S. Army 1st Aero Squadron is operational.

1918: May 24, President Woodrow Wilson creates the Army Air Service in response to the growth of military air power during World War I.

1926: July 2, the Air Service is redesignated as the Army Air Corps.

1939–1945: The Second World War transforms U.S. military aviation.

1941: June 20, the United States Army Air Force (USAAF) is created and becomes the largest air force in the world by 1944.

1947: September 18, the United States Air Force (USAF) is formed, officially a separate unit from the U.S. Army; October 14, USAF test pilot Chuck Yeager flies his Bell XS-1 at more than the speed of sound, the world's first supersonic flight.

1961–1975: The USAF becomes involved in the Vietnam War; it loses over 2,000 aircraft during the conflict and conducts some of the heaviest bombing raids in history.

1980s: The USAF conducts regular military operations in several places, including Grenada (1983), Libya (1986), and Panama (1989).

1990–1991: The Gulf War; the USAF plays a dominant role in destroying Iraqi military forces and supporting Allied operations.

1992–1998: USAF combat aircraft and humanitarian flights perform hundreds of missions in the former Yugoslavia.

2001–2014: Following the attacks against the United States on September 11, the USAF conducts operations as part of the war against terrorism, particularly in Afghanistan.

2004–present: Air strikes aid in northwest Pakistan.

2010–present: Air strikes against suspected Al Qaeda and al Shabaab positions in Yemen.

2014–present: U.S. Air Force completes humanitarian air drop in Iraq.

Further Resources

Websites

The USAF's own website: www.af.mil/

Information about USAF careers, see: www.airforce.com/

The USAF Museum: www.wpafb.af.mil/museum/

The Air National Guard: www.ang.af.mil/

The USAF ROTC: https://www.afrotc.com/

Further Reading

Archer, Bob. *U.S. Air Force: The New Century.* North Branch: MN: North Branch: Midland. 2001.

Basel, G.I. *Pak Six: A Story of the War in the Skies of North Vietnam.* New York, NY: Jove Publications, 1992.

Boyne, Walter J. *Beyond the Wild Blue: A History of the United States Air Force 1947–1997.* New York, NY: St. Martin's Press, 1997.

Brehm, Jack, and Pete Nelson. *That Others May Live: The True Story of the PJs, Real Life Heroes of the Perfect Storm.* New York, NY: Three Rivers Press, 2001.

Donald, David, ed. *U.S. Air Force Air Power Directory.* Westport, CT: Airtime Publishing, 1992.

Hearn, Chester G., and Robert F. Dorr. *Air Force: An Illustrated History.* Minneapolis, MN: Zenith Press, 2015.

Morse, Stan. *Gulf Air War Debrief.* Westport, CT: Airtime Publishing, 1991.

U.S. *Air Force Survival Guide.* New York, NY: Skyhorse Publishing, 2008.

U.S. *Department of the Air Force Handbook.* New York, NY: International Business Publications, 2000.

Wright, Stephen E. *Air Force Officer's Guide.* Mechanicsburg, PA: Stackpole Books, 2014.

Index

About the Author

Dr. Chris McNab has written and edited numerous books on military history and the world's elite military forces. His list of publications to date includes *The Illustrated History of the Vietnam War, German Paratroopers of World War II, The World's Best Soldiers, The Elite Forces Manual of Endurance Techniques,* and *How to Pass the SAS Selection Course.* Chris's research into these titles has brought him into contact with many of the world's elite units, including the U.S. Marines and British Special Forces. Chris has also contributed to the field of military technology with publications such as *Weapons of War: AK47, Twentieth-Century Small Arms,* and *Modern Military Uniforms.* His editorial projects include *The Battle of Britain* and *Fighting Techniques of the U.S. Marines 1941–45.* Chris lives in South Wales, United Kingdom.

About the Consultant

Manny Gomez, an expert on terrorism and security, is President of MG Security Services and a former Principal Relief Supervisor and Special Agent with the FBI. He investigated terrorism and espionage cases as an agent in the National Security Division. He was a certified undercover agent and successfully completed Agent Survival School. Chairman of the Board of the National Law Enforcement Association (NLEA), Manny is also a former Sergeant in the New York Police Department (NYPD) where he supervised patrol and investigative activities of numerous police officers, detectives and civilian personnel. Mr. Gomez worked as a uniformed and plainclothes officer in combating narcotics trafficking, violent crimes, and quality of life concerns. He has executed over 100 arrests and received Departmental recognition on eight separate occasions. Mr. Gomez has a Bachelor's Degree and Master's Degree and is a graduate of Fordham University School of Law where he was on the Dean's list. He is admitted to the New York and New Jersey Bar. He served honorably in the United States Marine Corps infantry.